The Isle of Mists

D0109960

A Magical World Awaits You
Read

★ THE ★
SECRETS
OF
DROON

THE SECRETS OF DROON

The Isle of Mists

by Tony Abbott
Illustrated by David Merrell
Cover illustration by Tim Jessell

A
LITTLE APPLE
PAPERBACK

SCHOLASTIC INC.
New York Toronto London Auckland Sydney
Mexico City New Delhi Hong Kong Buenos Aires

For the wonderful Walsh girls—
Maggie, Erin, Kayla, and their mom,
Margaret—the Upper World
will always have magic with you around.

No part of this publication may be reproduced in whole or in part,
or stored in a retrieval system, or transmitted in any form or by any means,
electronic, mechanical, photocopying, recording, or otherwise,
without written permission of the publisher.
For information regarding permission, write to Scholastic Inc.,
Attention: Permissions Department, 557 Broadway, New York, NY 10012.

ISBN 0-439-56048-9

Text copyright © 2004 by Robert T. Abbott.
Illustrations copyright © 2004 by Scholastic Inc.

All rights reserved. Published by Scholastic Inc.
SCHOLASTIC, LITTLE APPLE, and associated logos
are trademarks and/or registered trademarks of Scholastic Inc.

12 11 10 9 8 7 6 5 4 3 2 1   4 5 6 7 8 9/0

Printed in the U.S.A.   40
First printing, July 2004

Contents

One

It's Just About Time

Eric Hinkle shivered in his tiny hiding place.

His elbows were bent over his head; his legs were bunched up tightly beneath him.

He was all twisted and couldn't move.

But that wasn't the worst part.

Thump-thump! Footsteps were getting closer.

Someone was coming for him.

I am soooo trapped, he thought. *I should probably just yell for help. I should!*

But Eric didn't yell for help.

He smiled instead.

I'm always in a tight spot like this! he thought. *This is like every adventure I've ever been on. Every adventure in Droon, that is —*

Droon!

That was the world of mystery and magic he and his best friends, Julie Rubin and Neal Kroger, had found one day under his basement stairs.

It was an amazing land of gleaming cities, castle-topped mountains, and serpent-filled seas.

Thump-thump . . . The footsteps slowed.

Whenever Eric thought about Droon, his heart swelled. He had made incredible friends there. On their first adventure, he had met Keeah, a young princess and wizard.

Keeah could blast violet sparks from her fingertips. She knew tons of magical spells, all taught to her by Galen Longbeard, the greatest wizard in Droon. Now that Galen was away on a long journey, her powers were growing stronger all by themselves.

Together with Keeah and her parents, King Zello and Queen Relna, and Max, a spunky spider troll, Eric, Julie, and Neal had helped keep most of Droon safe from the clutches of Lord Sparr.

Sparr! thought Eric. *Wickedest of wicked sorcerers!*

For ages, Sparr had tried to conquer Droon for himself. Now that he had collected his legendary Three Powers, there was almost nothing stopping him and his nasty Ninns from taking over.

Ungh! Eric tried to move his toes, but couldn't.

Even though he and his friends loved the awesome adventures in Droon, Eric knew that long, long ago the Upper World had been filled with magic, too. At least it was, until a time-traveling thorn princess named Salamandra stole it and disappeared into Droon.

Now magic was almost gone from his world.

Eric smiled again.

Almost.

Zzzz! His hands blazed with sudden silver sparks, lighting up the small space.

"Cut it out, Eric, or our teacher will find us in this closet!"

Closet? Teacher?

Eric winced. So, okay, he wasn't exactly on a big adventure in Droon right then. He was squished in the school supply closet with Julie.

But it was true about the sparks!

Eric could shoot bright silver beams from his fingertips anytime he wanted. And sometimes even when he didn't.

"Sorry, Julie," he whispered. "I've been sparking like crazy all day. That's why I hid in here. My sparks went off in the hall just as a class was coming, and I didn't want them to see me. I think something big is coming. I can feel it."

"I can't feel anything," she said. "I'm so squished, I may never be able to fly again!"

Eric chuckled. That was true, too. On a recent adventure, Julie had gained the ability to fly. In fact, that was why she was in the closet with him. Only minutes earlier, she had fluttered up off the hallway floor by accident, and had ducked inside to hide.

"Hold on a little longer, Julie," he urged. "It's just about time for school to be over —"

The footsteps stopped just outside the door.

Eric's fingers heated up. "Oh, no, please —"

The door whipped open, light flashed into the closet, and Eric tumbled out, scattering sparks everywhere. "Mrs. Michaels, we can explain!" he cried.

"It's not Mrs. Michaels we have to worry about!" said their friend, Neal, standing there shaking like a leaf. "Take a look at who's here!"

He pointed out the hall window at a silver object soaring over the school parking lot.

It was a flying ship. It had a giant dragon's head on the front. And at its wheel was a green-skinned teenager with wild thorns for hair.

"The dragon ship!" said Julie. "Salamandra!"

"The one and only," said Neal. "The last time we saw Miss Icky Hair, she was snitching magic all over Droon. Totally out of control!"

"She still needs driving lessons!" said Julie.

Whooom! The silver ship jerked toward the ground, then lurched up at the last second. A moment later they heard a crunch on the roof.

"Quick, let's get up there!" said Eric.

The three friends dashed out the hall doors to the school yard.

"I'll fly us up," said Julie. Glancing both ways to make sure no one was watching, she took the boys' hands and flew them all up to the roof.

The dragon ship teetered over the far edge.

At the wheel stood Salamandra, wobbling dizzily. Her cloak hung in tatters, her green skin looked pale, and her thorny hair was tangled in huge knots.

"Not bad!" she said. "For flying without a sail!"

Eric's hands sparked again. "How did you get here, Salamandra? *Why* are you even here?"

"Yeah," said Julie. "You already stole the magic out of our world. What more do you want?"

The thorn princess took a breath. "The dragon ship flew me from Droon's past to the future and back again. The ship flew so fast, it made my head spin —"

Neal laughed. "It tangled your hair, too!"

"My hair is tangled," she snapped, "because of what I saw! Sparr in a huge palace . . . the Golden Wasp at his side . . .

the Coiled Viper, too! I saw a black tower in the shape of a horn, all shiny and new, and blue fog streaking the sky. I heard strange, eerie howling —"

"Salamandra!" said Julie. "We've always been enemies. Why are you telling us this stuff?"

Salamandra flipped her thorny hair over her shoulders, her eyes flashing bright yellow. Eric thought she seemed very afraid.

"A new magic is rising in Droon. I'm sure of it," she said. "A kind of *supermagic*. Sparr wants it. A lot. I do, too —"

Neal made a face. "You don't need more magic, Salamandra. You need a comb!"

"I came to warn you!" she snarled. "If you don't want to get hurt, stay out of Droon!"

Eric trembled. "Sorry. We can't do that."

She flashed a smile. "Then put on your oven mitts, Droonlings, because things are heating up. Once I snitch the flag of Droon from Jaffa City as a sail for my ship, I'll fly anywhere I want. . . . ohhhhh!"

With an unexpected jerk, she fell to the ship's deck.

Kkkkk! A ring of orange flame crackled open in the sky. Then the dragon ship spun up off the roof and into the flame. It vanished in an instant.

Eric's heart raced. "I knew it. Sparr with all of his Three Powers. Blue fog. Weird sounds. Something big *is* happening!"

"If Salamandra plans to steal the royal flag, we need to warn Keeah now!" said Julie.

Fifteen minutes later, the three friends jumped off their school bus and rushed across Eric's yard to his house. They tossed their backpacks on the kitchen table, hurried down to the basement, and piled into a small closet under the stairs.

Julie closed the door behind them.

Neal reached to the ceiling light. He switched it off.

Whoosh! The floor disappeared. It became the top step of a rainbow-colored staircase, curving down and away from Eric's house.

All the way to Droon.

"This is always the absolute coolest thing," said Neal.

"I love it, too," agreed Julie. "Let's get moving."

One by one, the friends descended the stairs. They passed through feathery pink clouds and out over the deserted streets of a large city. The air was misty with the dew of early morning. A great gold-domed palace shone in the distance.

"Jaffa City," said Eric. Then he paused. "Listen. Salamandra tried to scare us so that we wouldn't come here. Well, she couldn't do that. But if she was right about what's going on, we need to be ready for anything —"

All of a sudden — *wumpeta-wumpeta!* — the sound of galloping hooves filled the morning air.

"Ho! Bring torches there!" a voice shouted below. "Quickly now!"

Julie gasped. "It's King Zello. Hurry to the bottom!"

They rushed down the stairs and onto a cobblestone street, just as the bearded king of Droon raced toward them on a shaggy, six-legged pilka. Behind him rode his wife, Queen Relna.

Trailing them both was Max, a flurry of paws and orange hair, unrolling a tattered scroll. "I know it's in this scroll somewhere! Dear Galen, where is it? Oh, children, you've come —"

"We had to," Eric blurted out. "Salamandra came to us —"

"Salamandra!" boomed Zello. "Not two minutes ago, she burst from a hole in the sky and stole our flag! But right now we have a bigger problem — we must stop *her*!"

A tiny girl in a blue dress and blond pigtails dashed down the far alley, giggling wildly.

Neal stopped. "You want to stop *her*? She looks like she's three years old. Why not just tell her it's nap time?"

"Because in six seconds, she'll climb to the top of the city wall," boomed Zello.

"And in nine seconds," said Max, still unrolling the scroll, "she'll trip on the steps and fall!"

At exactly that moment, the girl leaped up a narrow set of stairs aside the great city wall.

"How did you know that?" asked Julie.

"All this has happened before!" said

Relna, jumping from her pilka. "We know everything that little girl will do. That little girl . . . is Keeah!"

"What?" said Eric. "But that's impossible —"

A sudden a cry came from the stairs.

Everyone turned to see the little girl tumble backward.

She fell straight toward the ground.

Two

Man's Beast Friend

"Keeah!" cried Zello. Spurring his pilka, he raced to the wall.

"Found it!" whooped Max. "Galen's old charm. Read it, my queen!"

Relna snatched the scroll. *"Pimlo-imlo-sleeee!"*

There was a sudden flash of light, then — *floop!* — Keeah dropped gently into her father's arms, no longer a tiny girl, but her full-size, normal princess self.

"My Keeah!" boomed Zello. "You're *you* again!"

"We were so afraid," said Relna, giving her daughter a hug.

Keeah hugged them back. "I'm fine. And glad to be me!"

"Whew!" Max sighed, rolling up the scroll again. "My master wrote his ancient charms backward, but sometimes they are just the thing!"

Neal blinked at his friends, then frowned at Keeah. "Wait a second. I don't get it. That little girl really *was* you?"

Keeah took a breath and nodded. "It happened this morning. A strange blue fog came in my window. Suddenly I was three again —"

Eric gulped. "Blue fog! Salamandra told us about that. Are you saying it made you *younger?*"

"Not only Keeah," said Zello. "I woke

up yesterday with no beard. No one recognized me. They even refused to serve me the king's breakfast."

Neal's eyes bulged. "That's extremely harsh."

"Tell me about it," said the king. "Luckily, we found Galen's old scroll. My beard was back by lunch!"

"This is so weird," mumbled Julie. "Salamandra warned us about crazy stuff happening."

"She even told us she was going to steal the flag," said Eric.

Keeah nodded. "She did steal it. We'll show you."

Five minutes later, they were on the wall overlooking the palace. The royal square was beautiful in the early dawn, except for one thing. The big empty hole where the flagpole of Droon had once stood.

"Salamandra stole it, then drove the dragon ship away in a ring of flames before we could stop her," said Max.

The kids remembered how after the mysterious flying ship was built, Galen took it apart and hid the pieces. Jaffa City's flagpole was the ship's mast. The beautiful flag of Droon was its main sail.

"Now we have no idea where Salamandra is," said Relna.

Keeah put up her hand. "Wait. Listen to that!"

Roooww-ooww! An eerie cry echoed over the city.

Julie glanced at Eric and Neal. "Howling. Salamandra told us about that, too."

All at once, something leaped over the outer wall in a single bound and raced right through the empty streets. The creature had rough, gray skin and was shaped like a large dog.

A large dog with two heads.

"Holy cow," said Eric. "It's Kem. Sparr's pet."

Neal grunted. "Pet? No way. My dog Snorky's a pet. Kem is some kind of monster beastie thing!"

"And if Sparr sent him, he is up to no good," said Max. "What do you say we spy on him?"

Together, they scurried carefully along the wall and peered over. Kem trotted to the hole where the flagpole used to be. He sniffed for a moment, then lifted one head and held it perfectly still.

"What is he doing?" whispered Julie.

The second head lifted up next to the first.

Both sets of eyes stared out over the walls.

"He's pointing!" said Relna.

"Snorky could do that if he wanted to," added Neal.

Zello frowned. "So! Kem is not just a nasty watchdog, he is Sparr's nasty hunting dog, too."

"He must be hunting for the dragon ship," said Eric.

Rooooww-ooww! Kem broke from his pose and ran in the direction he had pointed. With another easy leap, he was up over the outer wall of the city and onto the plains at a hard run.

Max tucked Galen's tattered scroll into a pouch on his belt. "Kem is going east. We must follow him. With any luck, he'll lead us right to the flying ship."

"And to Sparr," said Keeah. "He wants the ship most of all."

Sparr did want the dragon ship. And everyone knew why.

Long ago, in the shadowy past of

Droon, a creature named Ko once ruled an empire of fearsome beasts. A beast himself with four arms, three eyes, and the head of a bull, Ko taught Sparr his dark magic, turning the young son of a great wizard into the most dangerous of sorcerers.

After years of struggle, Galen defeated Ko. Legend said that when Ko was near death, the dragon ship would fly him home to the place he was born.

Eric spoke its name. "The Isle of Mists."

"The Isle of Mists," Keeah repeated. "It's said to have the most powerful magic ever seen."

"*Supermagic?*" asked Julie. "Salamandra said a new power was rising in Droon. Do you think she was talking about the Isle of Mists?"

Neal gulped. "But, come on. That's just a weird old legend, right?"

"A legend perhaps," said Relna. "But if

Ko's ancient palace does exist, there's only one place it can be —"

"In the Serpent Sea," said Zello. "Keeah, you go with Max and our friends to follow Kem. We'll sail to the Serpent Sea. If the Isle of Mists is real, we shall find it, and get to the bottom of this!"

Neal snorted. "Something tells me when we get to the bottom, we'll probably find Sparr there, and his creepy dog, too!"

The king and queen hugged Keeah, then hurried to the dock, where the royal ship, *Jaffa Wind*, sat ready to sail.

Eric watched as it quickly left the city's port for the open sea.

Was the Isle of Mists a legend like the gold at the end of the rainbow? he wondered. *Or the Fountain of Youth?*

Or was the Isle of Mists real?

He turned. "Guys, I was only half right when I said we should be ready for anything. Today, I think we need to be ready for *everything*!"

"I know I am," said Keeah. "Come on. Follow that howling dog!"

They rushed to the stables, mounted their pilkas, and galloped through the square where the flag of Droon had just waved.

As they roared out of the city gates, Kem raced on ahead, a tall plume of dust coiling up over the plains.

Three

The Wonderful Wonder

The pilkas rode hard after Kem. Three times the dog stopped, changed direction, and raced away again howling — *row-oooo!*

"It's almost like he's talking," said Neal.

Max spurred his pilka up a low hill. "He is talking, only not to us. He's signaling to Sparr where the dragon ship is."

"Should I fly after him?" asked Julie.

"You don't have to," said Keeah. She pulled her reins at the top of the hill. Her pilka stopped. "Kem is slowing down. Look there."

In a valley below them lay a tiny village of green huts shaped like mushrooms. Each had a small grass yard and a big round door. Four plump towers squatted gaily around a main square.

"It's so beautiful and fun-looking," said Julie.

"It looks like a theme park," said Neal.

Eric thought so, too. He couldn't forget Salamandra's warning — *if you don't want to get hurt, stay out of Droon* — but gazing down on the little village made him glad he had come.

"Who lives there?" he asked.

"The Orkins," said Keeah.

The Orkins. They all knew the story of

the gentle blue creatures. Tower builders and cheese makers, fun-loving and playful, the Orkins were among the very earliest of Droon's people. For ages they had kept to themselves in their little world of peace and quiet.

And then Emperor Ko found them.

Ko forced the Orkins to build palaces for him. Over time, his dark magic transformed the skilled blue builders into clumsy red warriors.

Every cheerful Orkin had become a very uncheerful Ninn.

That's how the Ninns came to be.

"The village looks deserted," said Julie.

"But if Kem is tracking Salamandra, why would he come here?" asked Eric. "Once Salamandra stole the Droon flag, she could fly anywhere. She said so herself. Why come to the little Orkin village?"

Keeah turned. "I don't know. Maybe

she saw something in the future that made her fly here. Let's find out."

"On foot and quietly," added Max. "Remember, Kem has four ears!"

The children slid off their pilkas and crept down toward the village. When they got there, the two-headed dog was padding softly between the towers, both heads still searching the sky.

"This place is so strange," whispered Julie. "I know we're following Kem, but suddenly I feel like playing!"

Neal darted up to a house and peered around it. "When I play with Snorky he doesn't find flying ships, just creepy old bones! He'd love this funny village, though."

Keeah smiled. "The Orkins aren't really magical, but visitors here always feel happy."

Eric remembered the first time he and his friends had ever seen an Orkin. They were surrounded by a bunch of angry

Ninns, when all of a sudden, the red warriors discovered their past.

What happened was amazing.

Ploink! A fierce Ninn became a playful Orkin, right before their eyes. Then another changed, and another. A whole troop of Ninns returned to their true Orkin selves. When they went back to their village, it rose from ruins to become beautiful and happy again.

"It must be something in the air," said Eric.

Max chuckled. "But hush, please, or Kem will start hunting *us*!"

Sparr's dog slowed in the main square. The five friends huddled quietly at the base of the tallest tower and peeked around.

Kem was pointing again.

"That pointing creeps me out," whispered Neal.

There was a sudden noise behind them, and a voice said, "All of you are *it*!"

Spinning around, the children saw the round face, soft chin, and large smile of a plump blue creature floating just above them.

Eric gasped. "An Orkin!"

"Welcome to our village, everyone!" the Orkin said. Letting go of a long springy rope that hung from the tower's top, he landed with a soft *plumf*!

"My name is Djambo! All my brothers and sisters are playing hide-and-seek. They're doing the hiding part, of course, and I'm doing the —"

"Shhh!" the children hissed, and yanked Djambo behind the tower.

"We're trying to hide, too!" whispered Keeah. She quickly explained how Kem had tracked Salamandra to his village.

His eyes widening, Djambo peered around the tower. "I love doggies! And this one has an extra head to pet —"

"Don't pet either one," said Neal. "He's Sparr's dog —"

Roowwwooo! Kem howled loudly.

"And here it comes," said Eric. "Here comes the ship!"

The sky crackled, a giant ring of flame appeared, and the dragon ship spun wildly out of it. At the same time, a bolt of red lightning exploded over the ship's bow — *ka-blammm!*

"Red lightning?" cried Julie. "Sparr must be here, too!"

Rocked by the blast, the ship dropped to the ground, thudding down in a nearby yard. Salamandra spilled out.

"Well, that was rough —" she said.

Clack . . . clack . . .

Lord Sparr himself stepped from behind one of the other towers and made his way slowly across the square. A cloak as black and glistening as a crow's feathers was wrapped around him. The jagged fins behind his ears glowed a brilliant red. In one gloved hand, Sparr held a smoking red jewel. It was the Red Eye of Dawn, the first of his magical Three Powers. He raised his other hand to Kem.

"Who's a good Kem to find Daddy's dragon ship?" he asked.

"At least he is nice to his doggy," whispered Djambo.

Salamandra sneered. "And who's a bad Sparr to knock me out of the sky?"

Sparr laughed. "Princess Salamandra! The last time we fought, you had me trapped. Now it looks like the shoe is on the other foot."

"Speaking of shoes," said Salamandra, "you're in the same moldy outfit as always. Is it what they're wearing on . . . the Isle of Mists?"

At the mention of the Isle of Mists, Sparr grinned icily. Then he opened his cloak and removed from it a large golden crown.

"The Coiled Viper!" whispered Keeah.

The crown was shaped like a snake twisted upon itself and ready to strike. Its arched head was made to hold two blue jewels.

Only one of them was in the Viper's head.

Galen had hidden the other jeweled eye.

Salamandra squinted at the crown. "You've been *testing* the Viper, haven't you? You want to see if it really works, don't you?"

"Testing? What does she mean?" whispered Keeah.

"Soon, my little tests will be over, and you'll see my crown complete," said Sparr. "Or maybe you won't — *if you aren't here*!"

He snapped his fingers and a high-pitched buzzing sound filled the air — *zzzzzt!* A few moments later, the bright gold wings and stingers of a giant flying creature appeared over the nearby hill.

"The Golden Wasp!" gasped Max. "Ugly bug! Sparr has all Three Powers now!"

At Sparr's command, the Wasp swooped quickly at the princess and forced her away from the ship.

The sorcerer laughed. "Buh-bye, Salamandra!"

"You think you've seen the last of me?" snarled the princess. "Well, nunh-unh!" She ran from house to house, chased by the Wasp, finally disappearing over the hill.

Sparr turned. "Now, Kem, our own journey begins! On board!"

Together, they hopped onto the dragon ship. Holding the Red Eye high, Sparr mumbled a few words. A red wind spun out of the jewel and filled the great flag of Droon. The ship rose up.

"He's getting away!" cried Max. "We have to follow him —"

Djambo grinned. "I know a way! The Orkin Wonder! It's so much fun!"

As the dragon ship stretched its wings and sailed higher, Djambo jumped up and grabbed the rope hanging from the tower's top.

"Behold the Orkin Wonder," he said. "Cheese!"

The kids stared at the long rope of cheese dangling down.

"String cheese?" said Neal. "String cheese will help us?"

Djambo laughed. "We prefer to call it *spring* cheese! Grab hold, pull hard, and *boing* you go. Up, up, up to the dragon ship!"

Max jumped nervously. "Sparr is nearly gone!"

Keeah frowned, then shrugged. "All right, everyone, grab some cheese!"

Each of them took hold of the Orkin Wonder and pulled away from the tower.

"More . . . more . . . and more!" said Djambo, tugging the cheese with all his might. "Even more!"

They pulled the cheese until it became very thin.

Finally, the cheese began to pull back.

"Oh, man!" cried Eric. "Here — we — go!"

Fwing! The Orkin Wonder shot them

up from the ground, right over the tower, and straight through the air.

Ploing . . . oing . . . oing . . . oing-g-g-g!

All the way through the wispy pink clouds they flew.

And right up to the dragon ship.

Four

All Aboard!

The six friends were flung into a heap at the back of the ship. *Plop-op-op-op!*

Sparr and Kem didn't turn from the wheel.

"They didn't even hear us!" whispered Keeah, huddling low. "The storm was making too much noise."

"And now we're stowaways!" chirped Max.

Crouching as low as possible, they hid from sight. The Wasp was back from chasing away Salamandra. It weaved back and forth behind the ship, searching the skies.

"That Wasp totally creeps me out!" whispered Neal.

Julie frowned. "What *doesn't* creep you out?"

Neal licked his fingers. "Well, the cheese —"

Sparr spun the wheel and drove the ship lower, circling over a great desert. Sand dunes rolled on and on below them, ending finally at the foot of a pink mountain range.

"I thought this was a nonstop flight to the Isle of Mists," said Eric. "But we're going down. It looks like Sparr's getting ready to land."

The monster dog strained its necks over the bow, pointing to more than a hundred

Ninns in black battle armor tramping across the sand.

"Ninns," whispered Djambo. "They look tired. Do you think Sparr will give them a ride?"

Keeah grumbled softly as the ship flew lower. "That's not even the worst part. Sparr said the Viper would soon be complete. Well, what's the one thing he still needs?"

Eric turned to her. "You mean the Viper's other eye?"

Max nodded. "The last thing my master told us was to keep the jewel moving so Sparr wouldn't find it. Well, Sparr has found it."

Keeah pointed to a caravan of pilkas snaking its way over the dunes not far away. As everyone watched, the caravan looped once, backtracked, went sideways, then circled some palm trees near a camp of colorful tents.

"What a fun way to travel!" said Djambo.

"That caravan is carrying the eye," said Keeah. "And as you can tell from the way it travels, its captain is . . . Nelag."

"Nelag?" Julie blinked. "Uh-oh."

Nelag was the double of Galen, charmed to take his place whenever the old wizard was away. But Nelag had no real power. He turned out to be the opposite of Galen in every way.

Even his name was backward.

The dragon ship dipped once more, then skimmed along the ground, spraying sand behind it. The instant it stopped, Sparr charged from the ship. "I need the eye!" he shouted.

"Quick, everyone. This is our stop,

too!" said Eric. "Get to Nelag before Sparr does!"

They jumped out and raced behind a giant sand dune, meeting Nelag just as his caravan entered the campsite.

"Ho-ho! Princess, children," the pretend wizard giggled as he jumped from his pilka. "I've hidden the jewel. Now watch me fool Sparr!"

"But Nelag —" Max started.

Even as the sorcerer raced toward them, Nelag swished his robes in one direction, then another, twirled on his heels, dipped, jumped, and finally lurched backward between the tents.

Djambo laughed. "You're already fooling *us*!"

But Sparr was too quick. He blasted the tents away one by one — *blam-blam-blam!* — until he trapped the friends under the high trees.

Raising his sparking hands to them, Sparr smiled coldly. "Junior wizards," he sneered. "I wondered how long it would take before you got in my way."

"Too long, Sparr," said Keeah, standing firm.

"But better late than never —" added Eric. "Keeah, now —"

Bla-blam! Two blasts sprang from their fingers.

Sparr dodged the beams, then flung a powerful red bolt at the children, toppling them to the sand.

"Ninns!" he shouted. An instant later, his troop of red warriors clambered over the dunes. Each one pulled out a jagged sword and waved it fiercely at the friends, forcing them back.

"Nelag, give me the Viper's eye," said Sparr calmly.

"You'll never find it here!" said the pretend wizard. At once, he fell to the sand and began digging a hole.

Sparr smiled. "You're right, my opposite friend. I won't find the jewel down there." He floated off the dune and into the palm tree overhead. He came down clutching a small wooden box in his hands.

"Oh, no . . ." grumbled Max.

Nelag stopped digging and covered his ears. "Careful! That box is booby-trapped. With Fizzling Fizzler Fireworks!"

Sparr opened the lid anyway.

Zing! A single pink spark flashed up in his face, struck him on the chest, fizzled for a second, then went out. *Phut-t-t-t-t-t.*

Eric groaned. "Well, that didn't work —"

"But Fizzlers worked when Galen made them," said Nelag. "Four hundred years ago."

"Fizzling Fizzlers, indeed. Nothing but a dud!" said Sparr. He plucked out a small blue jewel and flung the box to the sand. "Kem, look. The Viper's eye is mine at last! Ninns, to the ship. You others — buh-bye!"

Blasting the sand once more, Sparr leaped back to the ship. His red warriors tumbled onboard after him. *Whooom!* The dragon ship lifted from the sand and began to rise toward the sparkling mountains.

"Ten degrees south!" Sparr cried. "Make a course into the flames! And to the Serpent Sea!"

"He's getting away!" cried Neal.

"I can fly after him," said Julie.

"Maybe one of Galen's backward spells will stop him!" said Max.

Nelag took the scroll, then tucked it in his belt. "I have a better idea. Rockets for each of us. And they really work. Honest!" He emptied his pilka's saddlebags and handed out rocket-shaped fireworks two feet long. "Come now. Sit on them. Keeah, a spark, if you please!"

After everyone sat on a rocket, Keeah sent a spark to each rocket's fuse. "Okay, but . . ."

Fwooooosh! — the rockets shot up from the ground and zigzagged together to the dragon ship.

"Awesome!" yelled Neal, clutching his rocket tightly. "They actually work. We're flying!"

Eric leaned into his rocket, urging it to go higher and faster. "And we're gaining on him! Come on, rocket, to the ship! Fly!"

Kem saw them first and howled. *Rooo-oowww!*

"Still there, troublemakers?" snarled Sparr. "Too bad it looks like stormy weather for you!"

As they approached the ship, the sor-cerer raised the Red Eye of Dawn. A sud-

den stormy swirl burst from it, pouring torrents of rain over the friends.

"It's raining, it's pouring! And you're falling!" laughed Sparr.

As the dragon ship wove up into the air and the rain fell harder, Nelag's rockets flickered and sputtered. Then they died.

Almost the last thing Eric saw before the rockets fell was the Coiled Viper, both eyes gleaming, glowing with light from head to tail.

Almost.

The *very* last thing he saw was a puff of blue fog streaking out from the Viper's eyes.

"Holy *smoke*!" cried Eric.

That's when the rockets fell.

Five

Leaf It to Keeah

"Noooo!" cried Neal. "Somebody do something!"

Even as they dropped straight down, Max spun a tight silken web and flung it up. It filled with air like a parachute.

"Grab on!" he shouted. "It will slow our fall!"

Everyone jumped for the web and held tight. Nelag leaped from his falling rocket straight through a streak of blue fog.

By the time Max's silky web floated onto the pink cliffs and the friends rolled softly to the ground, the fog had vanished.

And so had Nelag.

Plop! Plop! His two silver slippers dropped from the sky, one after the other. And that was all. Nelag himself was nowhere.

Keeah rushed to the slippers. "Oh, no. Nelag?"

"What happened to our friend?" cried Max. "Where did he go?"

"I hope he's not hurt," added Djambo. "I just met him!"

Eric stared at the slippers. "I think he's okay."

Everyone turned to him as the fog drifted away and vanished.

Eric took a deep breath. "Okay, look," he said. "Nelag went through the blue fog. But so far, it hasn't actually hurt anyone, right? I mean, it made you younger, Keeah. Your father, too. Maybe the Viper really just made Nelag younger, too. I mean, how old is he?"

"Of course!" said Keeah. "Galen created the charm for Nelag only a few years ago. If the blue fog turned him back even three years, he would vanish completely."

"Poor guy," said Neal, tucking the silver slippers in his belt. "So young, he's not even here. And since the scroll vanished with him, we can't try a spell on him."

Eric nodded. "Only the Viper can bring him back now —"

Kkkk-kkk! Bolt after bolt of lightning flashed, and the storm from the Red Eye of Dawn drove the dragon ship toward the distant clouds.

"All the more reason to follow Sparr," said Julie. "I can still track him and make sure he doesn't try any more tricks along the way. This is my chance to use my powers to help."

With every passing second, the silvery glint of the dragon ship was getting smaller.

Keeah and Eric shared a look. Finally, Keeah said, "Julie, be really, really careful."

Julie smiled. "Always!"

Putting her hands together, she launched herself into the air. She looped over the pink mountains like a bird and flew right toward Sparr's ship.

Djambo watched her fly. "She'll do it. I know she will."

"I hope so," said Eric. "If Salamandra is right — and she's been right so far — Sparr will find the Isle of Mists."

"If it exists," muttered Neal.

"We need to pretend it does," said Keeah. "Come on, everyone. Down the mountain, through the forest, and to the Serpent Sea. And the quicker the better!"

It took nearly an hour to slide down the pink cliffs. Next, they trekked into a jungle of giant trees. Finding a path at last, the friends wormed down the steep mountain. Suddenly, Keeah put up her hand and stopped.

A wild river crossed the path. It raced along for a while, then dropped off, crashing fifty feet to the open sea below.

"Waterfall," Max grumbled.

Eric looked down at the raging water. White-topped waves rose and crashed loudly. "Uh . . . I'm not sure about this," he said.

"I'm pretty sure about it," said Neal. "I'm pretty sure we need to find another way down —"

Kawww! Kawww!

Without warning, two large birds flapped over the treetops. They had scales, and spikes sticking out of their heads. Their bright red eyes searched the ground below.

"Those are ancient birds, centuries old!" said Djambo. "Where did *they* come from?"

"From the blue fog?" asked Eric.

"It's where they're coming *to* that worries me," said Keeah. "And they're coming to *us*! Hide —"

But just as they tried to run, there was a sudden crackle of twigs, a flash of yellow across the path, and — *floomp!* — a giant leaf crashed from the trees above and trapped them completely.

"Hey, let us out —" cried Neal.

"No," whispered Keeah. "Hush. Stay still!"

Kaww-kaww! The giant birds dived for the ground. The friends heard them flapping nearer and nearer, circling the river.

A minute later, there was nothing.

Max carefully poked his head out from under the leaf. "The birds are leaving," he whispered. "We're safe."

Djambo flipped the leaf over.

"Nice of them not to stay for lunch," said Neal.

Eric watched the birds fly away over the distant trees. Then he glanced into the forest. He was almost certain he had seen a pair of eyes just before the leaf fell — piercing yellow eyes — but now there was no one. "I don't like this place. We need to get out of here. Fast."

"The fastest way is down the river," said Keeah. She looked at the leaf and grinned. "I admit it's not the *Jaffa Wind* or a flying ship, but this leaf just might float."

"Float?" said Neal. "No way am I going down the waterfall on that!"

Djambo dragged the giant leaf to the

edge of the river and slid it in. "Are you staying behind then, Neal?"

Neal frowned. "I don't like waterfalls. But I don't like being alone, either. I'm in!"

He hopped in, followed by Max, Keeah, Djambo, and finally Eric. Pulling branches from the riverside for oars, they pushed off.

Right away, the current drew them in.

Waves tossed the leaf, gathering speed until the friends were swept straight for the waterfall. In a moment, the leaf was tossed over the edge.

Eric tightly clutched the leaf. "Whoaaa!"

For a few moments they were airborne, then — *splooosh!* — the leaf struck the river below, nearly going under.

"Yahoo!" cried Djambo. "It worked!"

"I think I love waterfalls!" said Neal, grinning with excitement.

Five minutes later, the river pushed them out to the open sea.

Ten minutes after that, they glimpsed another flying figure soaring above them. This time, it wasn't an ancient bird.

"Julie!" cried Djambo, waving his arms. "Over here!"

Julie dived through the clouds and soon lighted on the leaf between Keeah and Max, her eyes gleaming with excitement.

"Wow, you are such an expert flyer now!" said Neal.

"Thanks," she said, trying to catch her breath. "Okay. There's good news and bad news. The dragon ship escaped into one of those orange flame holes and vanished. I totally lost Sparr."

"So what's the good news?" asked Eric.

Julie sighed. "*That*'s the good news. The bad news is that a gigantic storm came out of nowhere. It's full of thunder and red lightning. And it makes a hurricane look like a sprinkle!"

"Out of nowhere?" said Keeah. "Oh, my gosh, that's it!"

"What do you mean?" asked Neal.

Keeah started rowing harder. "Sparr is using the Red Eye of Dawn to hide the very thing we're looking for. The thing not on any map. The place no one could ever find!"

Max gulped. "Oh, dear. The Isle of Mists?"

"The Isle of Mists," said Keeah. "Come on!"

As they rowed faster, the giant storm came into view.

"There is no Isle of Mists," Neal moaned. "There is no —"

Suddenly, the storm became huge.

Whoo-oo-oosh! — a powerful wind swept over them and sucked the leaf into a giant funnel of water.

After what seemed like an eternity of spinning wind and crashing waves, the leaf bobbed out onto water as thick and black as oil.

Everyone looked around.

A whirling wall of water hundreds of feet high surrounded them. But they drifted calmly in the center.

They were *inside* the storm.

"This is much better," said Djambo.

"We hope," said Keeah.

A heavy mist, as thick and gray as dirty cotton, rolled over the dark waves. When it parted for a moment, they saw it.

In the distance was a long shape rising above the water.

It was high in the middle and sloped down at the edges.

It was an island.

Julie swallowed loudly. "The Isle of Mists?"

"The Isle of Mists," said Djambo.

"So, okay," mumbled Neal, "maybe it does exist."

Mysterious Island of Mystery

As the friends rowed toward the island, the mist thickened so they could barely see beyond their tiny boat. All of a sudden — *sloooo!* — a glint of silver cut across the sea just ahead of them.

"The d-dragon ship!" Max said with a shiver.

Hushed and slow, the magic ship moved over the black water. Sparr stood at the helm, his cloak wrapped tight, his eyes staring ahead. His army of Ninns huddled silently behind him.

On a stand in front of Sparr was the Coiled Viper, gleaming in its own light, poised as if it were ready to strike.

Eric's blood ran cold. He knew they would soon discover what the Viper was actually created for. He trembled to imagine what Sparr was really up to.

Thick fog swirled once more around the dragon ship, like the smoke of a snuffed candle, and it was gone.

"Okay, that was creepy," said Julie, rowing faster with her tree branch.

"Get ready for even more creepy," said Eric. "We're about to find the darkest magic ever."

Keeah nodded. "I hope my mother and father get here soon. We'll need as much help as possible."

Eric felt the same way. He remembered

how afraid Salamandra had seemed. And if *she* was scared about this place . . .

For twenty minutes more, they rowed toward the island.

Then Djambo spoke softly. "There," he said. "Look. . . ."

On the shore not twenty feet away lay the silver hull of the flying dragon ship.

It was leaning on the black sand.

It was empty.

"They landed," said Keeah. "Now it's our turn."

Giving a final push with their paddles, they urged their leaf to the dark shore.

It rode up onto the sand and stopped.

When they stepped from the leaf, their feet sank into the black sand with a soft *squish*.

"That's nice," said Neal, tugging his foot up. "I just remembered I left my hat in the boat."

"You weren't wearing a hat," said Djambo.

"You're right," said Neal. "Maybe I should take the boat and go shopping for one. But you guys go on. Start without me —"

Eric and Julie grabbed his arms.

"All for one and one for all," said Julie.

"All right . . . I'm coming . . . I'm coming. . . ."

As they made their way up the island, branches curled like fingers above them. Moss dripped down from the vines, brushing their shoulders. And here and there were traces of blue foggy air.

"Some light would be handy," said Max.

"Allow me," said Keeah. But the moment she raised her fingers, a violet beam shot out, looped sharply, and blasted the ground at her feet.

Splooog! Mud splashed up on her.

"Oh, yuck!" she groaned. "That didn't work!"

Eric flicked his fingers. *Zzzzeeeoooorr — splooog!*

He wiped mud from his face, too. "So, okay, then. That's one thing about the Isle of Mists. Wizard powers shoot back at themselves."

Neal grumbled. "We're in the total lair of the bad guy and we have no powers? Just great!"

"But maybe it's a good thing that we're in the dark," said Max, pointing up the main hill of the island. "We certainly don't want *them* to see us."

A dozen campfires were scattered up the rising ground in front of them. Ninn warriors crouched near every fire, their red cheeks even redder in the flames' glow.

But instead of singing one of their usual

growly songs, the Ninns were strangely silent.

"My poor brothers," whispered Djambo. "Their faces show they are afraid of something. Very afraid."

"For once, I feel the same as the Ninns," said Neal.

"Salamandra was afraid, too," said Eric. "I think the thing we're all afraid of might be in there."

At the top of the hill was a giant mass of old battered walls and tumbled stones. Even through the hanging moss and mist, they could see carvings of winged and hoofed animals and statues of terrible beasts.

Above the ruins stood a black tower curving up from the soggy ground. It ended thirty feet high in a jagged, broken rim.

"If this is Ko's palace," whispered Julie, "I can't believe he was homesick for it."

As they crept closer, Eric felt his blood go cold. His heart pounded as he remembered what Salamandra had said.

I saw a black tower in the shape of a horn, all shiny and new.

"Salamandra must have been flying in the past if she saw this when it was new," he said.

"Four hundred years ago," said Keeah. "That's when Goll was destroyed and Ko's Empire of Shadows fell into ruin."

They crouched behind a large black stone. Up ahead, a band of heavily armed Ninns blocked a doorway at the foot of the palace.

The more Eric stared at the palace, the more he was sure light was coming from inside. "Sparr must be in there with the Viper."

Keeah grumbled. "Our powers are no

good here. How do we get past the Ninns?"

"Just don't ask me to tiptoe past them in Nelag's slippers!" whispered Neal.

Djambo giggled softly. "I wonder. . . . Long ago, Orkins were afraid of a creature called a striped bumbalo. Now we play a game. We imagine we hear a bumbalo growling, and we all run for cover. Then we eat cheese!"

Julie blinked. "Nice story, Djambo, but —"

"Since Ninns come from Orkins and Orkins from Ninns," Djambo continued, "to scare the Ninns away, just growl like a bumbalo!"

Everyone looked at him.

"A bumbalo," said Eric.

Djambo nodded excitedly. "A striped one!"

"What does a striped bumbalo sound like?" asked Keeah.

"Like this!" Djambo put his fingers in his mouth and breathed.

Eeee-gggg-arrrrr!

Suddenly, the Ninns stood up and stared into the distance.

Something moved in the swirling mist.

A moment later, a long furry tentacle thrust itself into the light.

"Uh, Djambo," said Max. "What's that?"

The Orkin looked thoughtful. "That looks like a gruffle. Funny it should be here. But then again, gruffles *do* like bumbalos."

Before they knew it, a huge spider with thick red legs and black fur loped out of the mist, trailing slimy white webbing behind it.

Oooooogggggg! the beast roared.

Eric gasped. "Djambo, when you say

gruffles *like* bumbalos, do you mean *are friends with*, or do you mean *want to eat?* For supper?"

Djambo scratched his chin. "More like lunch. Gruffles come from ancient Droon, you know —"

"Well, they should go back!" said Max. "Ahhhh!"

The spidery beast charged. Shrieking wildly, the Ninns bolted every which way across the hillside. They yelled and squealed, bumping into one another to get out of the way.

"Forget the gruffle!" shouted Keeah. "Now's our chance!" She jumped out of hiding and rushed up the hill.

As the friends charged through the tumbled stones, Neal turned to Eric. "You sure were right!"

"About what?" said Eric, leaping over a broken column.

"About being ready for *everything*!"

The next instant, Eric, Neal, Julie, Keeah, Max, and Djambo rushed into the darkness of Ko's palace.

The black, creepy, oh-so-smelly darkness.

Seven

Rock-a-bye Beastie

As the gruffle's cry faded away behind them, so did the confused yelling of the Ninns.

Swatting through cobwebs as thick as ropes, the six friends soon entered a great hall.

Or what had once been a great hall.

Splish! The broad stone floor was riddled with so many cracks that soupy water had risen from below into dark pools. Parts of the ceiling had tumbled down, and they could see the storm in the sky above. When lightning flashed, the room blazed with red light.

"Holy cow!" whispered Julie, waving at the mist.

"I know," agreed Neal. "How creepy can you get?"

Carved on the walls that were still standing were beastlike creatures, some with wings, some with hooves and fur, others with fins. Great thick columns, a few upright, many in pieces on the floor, were covered with pictures of more beasts.

And over everything wafted a stale breeze, sour and damp, pushing the mist first one way, then the other, back and forth across the hall.

"What *is* this place?" whispered Max.

Neal wrinkled his nose. "Wherever we are, I'd say it needs a good spring cleaning."

"Maybe the question isn't *where* we are," said Keeah, "but *when* we are. Look at this."

In front of her stood what looked like the remains of a bed. It had a little curved horn at each corner, railings on both sides, and rockers at the bottom.

"My gosh," said Julie. "That looks like a . . . a . . . cradle!"

Nearby was a serpent with a seat on its back and wheels instead of legs. It was tipped on its side, broken.

Djambo spun one of its wheels. "Friends, I believe we have found the legendary birthplace of Emperor Ko. This is where his terrible life began!"

"According to the legend," said Keeah, "it ended here, too —"

Keeah and Max passed between massive columns into a rounded chamber at the end of the room. Torches leaning out of the wall burned with mysterious red flames. Against the back of the chamber, and facing the main hall, was a throne of shiny black stone.

A colossal statue lay on the floor in front of it. It was shaped like an armored giant with a bull's head and four massive arms.

Max whimpered. "It's a statue of him. It's Ko."

"And now, it's no more than a crumbled-up wreck on the floor," said Neal. "Well, people, Sparr's supermagic is a supermess. There's nothing on the Isle of Mists but nothing!"

Staring at the fallen statue, Eric felt his neck tingle. The breeze blew past him. "Maybe," he said.

Julie turned. "What do you mean?"

He shook his head. "I don't know. This place *is* a mess. But if Sparr flew here to use the Viper, there's got to be a reason. I keep going back to what the Viper does. Keeah, when the blue fog touched you, you got younger, but nothing else around you did. . . ."

Keeah frowned. "Okay. But what do you mean . . . exactly?"

Eric felt the breeze coming through again, and his heart began to pound faster. "Exactly? I don't know. But maybe there's another way to look at this. Maybe the blue fog makes something from the past come back into our time. Like the young you and your younger father. And the creepy old birds. And the gruffle!"

"Something from the past?" whispered Neal. "Like supermagic?"

Everyone's mouth dropped. They turned and stared at the fallen statue. Eric took a step to join them, then stopped. He crouched to the floor. Amid the dust and broken stones was a small piece of black wood. It was carved in the shape of a bird. He picked it up.

Two little dots of green were painted above a long, narrow beak. It looked like a toy crow, he thought.

Lightning flashed again and the bird's green eyes seemed to glow brighter. Then, just as mist wafted over him again, he heard his name.

Errrricccc!

Suddenly, there was a scrape against the floor behind him. He jerked around to see a dim figure emerge slowly from the shadows.

"Salamandra!" said Keeah.

The thorn princess had changed from the last time they saw her. What was left of her cloak was no more than shredded cloth. One arm hung down at her side. Her green face was paler than ever. And she limped into the room.

"You're hurt," said Eric, rising from the floor.

She held up a hand. "Not enough to stop me!"

Eric saw that Salamandra's cruel smile was gone and that her eyes were tired. Her blazing yellow eyes.

Yellow. Just like the flash of yellow he thought he saw on the moutaintop.

He gasped. "It was you! You made the leaf drop! You saved us from those creepy birds. You were on the mountain with us —"

She waved her hand sharply. "I needed you to find the Isle of Mists. I helped you there. Then I followed you —"

"Wait a second," said Julie, scratching her nose and frowning. "When you came to our school this morning, you told us to stay out of Droon. But you didn't really want us to listen, did you? You wanted us to come!"

Salamandra stared at them one after another. Finally, she let out a breath. "If I hadn't given you all the clues and helped you along the way, you wouldn't be in this palace now. To see what Sparr will do —"

Neal shook his head. "I still don't get it. If Sparr's here for some supermagical thing, he'll be really bummed out. There's nothing left but rocking serpents —"

"He doesn't want a supermagical thing," said the thorn princess.

"What?" said Keeah.

"Not a *thing*!" Salamandra said. Then she turned, her eyes wild. "He's here — Sparr!"

With a swish of her tattered cloak, she was gone.

The next moment — *zzzzzt!* — the Golden Wasp flew into the chamber.

On its back sat Lord Sparr himself. His Red Eye of Dawn was blazing in one gloved hand, the Coiled Viper in the other.

He gazed at the children.

Slowly, he began to smile.

Eight

The Viper's Fangs

Zzzzzt! The Wasp hovered over the floor, its eyes flicking everywhere, staring at everything.

Hot blue sparks twinkled on Eric's fingertips.

"Oh, don't try that!" Sparr said, grinning as he slid to the floor. "You know that wizard powers are no good on the Isle. But just in case, I brought my army —"

He whistled sharply, and dozens of

Ninns jammed into the room, swords held high, grunting as they formed a fierce red wall.

"I guess they escaped the gruffle," said Julie.

"But they're still not happy," whispered Djambo. "Look at those sad faces!"

Sparr's fins darkened as he grinned at Keeah. "Your parents are caught in my storm, Princess. But if the Red Eye doesn't delay them, my Wasp will!"

He hissed briefly. "*Ssssrrrss!*"

The Wasp jerked back away through the halls.

Through the cracks in the ceiling above them, Eric saw the Wasp zooming into the red storm.

Keeah stared at Sparr. "You're already so evil. Whatever you hope to find here, you'd better think again —"

"Oh, I *have* thought again," Sparr

snapped. "Again and again and again! Since the very first time we met, when I found the Red Eye of Dawn after so long, all I have thought about is gathering my Three Powers again. Now that I have them, a great new adventure begins!"

A great new adventure? wondered Eric. *Meaning what?*

Sparr stepped slowly across the hall, toward the throne chamber. "Four centuries ago, the magical empire of Goll was defeated. Galen saw to that. Ko was wounded, and the dragon ship flew him here to the island where he was born —"

"Tell us something we don't know," said Neal.

"What you don't know," snapped Sparr, "is that in his final days, Ko summoned his greatest magic ever!"

Eric stared into the chamber. The wall flames moved first one way, then the other.

"Yes, Eric Hinkle. You know, don't you?" Sparr said quietly.

Keeah turned to her friend.

As he watched the flames flicker, Eric kept going over the clues Salamandra had given them.

Not a supermagical thing?

Not a *thing*.

No, he thought. *It couldn't be —*

"Tell us what you are thinking, Eric," said Sparr.

Eric swallowed hard. "The legend says that when Ko was near death, the dragon ship would bring him right here. But maybe . . . it's crazy . . . but Ko didn't come here to . . . you know . . . die. . . ?"

Neal laughed nervously. "Didn't come to die? Eric, did you eat the green part of the string cheese?"

"Go on," said Sparr, still grinning.

"I don't know, maybe Ko has been

waiting," Eric continued. "For four hundred years he's been waiting. For you. Maybe that old statue isn't really a statue. And that breeze . . ."

He paused as it wafted across the room and back again.

"It's not even a regular breeze, is it?" Eric said. "It's . . . breathing —"

"Yes! Yes! Correct!" crowed Sparr. "I knew you were special, Eric Hinkle! You've guessed it! Ko put himself into a deep slumber — *a four-century sleep!* — waiting for, oh, but you say it!"

Eric trembled. "Waiting for the Viper to go into the past . . . and bring Ko back again —"

"EXACTLY!" Sparr howled. He spun on his heels. "Now, Ninns, the time has come. My gloves will protect me, and I don't care about these children, but you need a charm. Stay behind this and you will be safe. *Kara-meloomna-sreee!*"

Zang! A veil of orange light appeared and settled over the Ninns.

Turning, Sparr raised the Coiled Viper in front of the statue. "And now, how does it go? Oh, yes! *Pleth-na-morlin-kananda-pelloh!*"

The Viper glowed with a sudden golden light.

Its jeweled eyes shone, and two jagged streaks of blue fog shot out from them. They curled around Sparr in larger and larger circles, sweeping over the Ninns and reaching at the friends.

"Don't let the fog touch us!" cried Keeah, diving to the floor, pulling Max and Julie with her.

Djambo yelped, "I like blue, but not blue fog!"

Neal and Eric dashed away from the misty fingers, leaping from one crumbled stone to another.

"Yes, run, run!" cried Sparr. "You can't escape the Viper's fangs! Time goes back, back, back!"

The storm of streaking blue fog was growing in the room.

"Neal, watch out!" yelled Julie. "Behind you!"

Arching back from a wisp of fog, Neal stumbled against a broken wall behind him, dropping Nelag's slippers to the floor. The mist came closer.

"I don't want to be three years old again!" said Neal. "I had weird hair! Get back!" Grabbing the slippers, he swatted wildly at the fog. "Back —"

The blue mist seemed to clutch at the slippers.

All of a sudden — *pooomf!* — something

in a long robe with silver trim shot out from Neal's hands.

It was Nelag! He tumbled to the floor, then jumped up holding the old battered scroll in his hands. "I'm ba-ackkk!"

"Holy cow!" Eric pulled the pretend wizard down behind a tumbled column. "I can't believe it! The Viper just took your slippers back in time. To when you were *you* —"

"Nelag, read the scroll!" said Keeah. "Or we'll all go to when there was no *us*!"

The pretend wizard whipped opened the scroll, giggled some backward words and — *ploomf!* — the kids were showered with orange light, too.

"Yay!" said Djambo. "We're saved —"

"Not quite," said Max. "Look . . . look. . . ."

As Sparr laughed and Kem howled, the friends stared through the cracked ceiling.

They saw the storm outside lessen and a pale sun appear. It slowed in the sky. Then it began to move the other way, edging across the clouds from west to east. Soon light and shadows streamed across the stones. The room went dark, then light, then dark again.

"The days are going backward!" said Djambo.

"Four hundred years," said Keeah, trembling. "To the day when Ko was awake!"

Seasons went by faster and faster. Years, decades, centuries!

Dust exploded from the floor. The crumbled stones rolled from where they had lain for centuries, then lifted up into place in the walls.

The palace was building itself back together!

When a nearby column shot upright, the friends jumped behind it.

Sparr laughed, raising the Viper even higher. "You cannot hide from this! Galen's victory is being undone. My magical crown goes back into the past for one single moment, and brings it forward to us. Ko — come to me!"

The room sparked and popped and crackled.

Even hidden, Eric felt his breath being sucked from him. If not for the spell, he felt as if they would all be drawn into the spinning wind.

Sparr braced himself. "Now, the great tower shall rise, and so shall Ko himself!"

The jagged tower did rise. Massive black stones shot up, course upon course, until the giant black horn was like new.

The blue fog spun faster and louder.

"Close your ears, everyone!" chirped Nelag. "My Fizzling Fizzler was four centuries old. It's now four centuries ago —"

"Ko!" cried Sparr, "Emperor! Rise up —
huh?"

KA-BOOOOM! A burst of pink sparks
exploded from Sparr's cloak, flying up into
his face.

"Ackggg!" he spun around and thudded
to the ground in a heap, twitching under
his cloak. His gloves flew off, and the Viper
fell, rolled across the floor, and stopped at
the statue.

The blue storm faded instantly.

"Hooray for Nelag and his Fizzler!"
whooped Julie.

"Not quite a dud after all!" Max
chirped.

Eric trembled as he peeked around the
column. "It doesn't matter. Look."

With a sound like stone grinding on
stone, the statue began to move. It raised
its giant bull's head from the floor. Its three

black eyes opened. And the friends knew it wasn't a statue anymore.

Slamming his great feet on the floor, Ko pushed with his four massive arms and rose up. He stood eight feet tall. His twin white tusks gleamed in the torchlight.

Then with a sound that shook the room, he bellowed.

"AAAAAARRRRRR!"

The ancient emperor of the beasts was awake.

Nine

The Black Horn

Flames shot from the tips of Ko's horns when he set the Coiled Viper on his head.

Whimpering, Kem crawled under his master's cloak, tugging it completely over both of them.

The Ninns stood under their orange veil, stunned and quaking.

At first, Ko's words sounded like the growling of an animal. *"Spar-r-r . . . graaah . . . thrrr . . ."*

Soon enough, real words sounded.

"Sparr!" said Ko, gazing at the lumpy cloth on the floor. "You did well to wake me. Now, come, Fintop and Grayclaws! Wake, old Witherbreath! Come, Snarly. The Empire of Goll begins anew. Soon, we will raise our black banners in Jaffa City!"

"Oh, no, please no," moaned Max, tugging on Keeah's sleeve.

"They won't!" she whispered.

The floors shook suddenly, and a creature thudded into the room. It was like a lion, only twice the size, with a fringe of spikes down its spine. It slapped eight gray paws on the floor.

"I saw his statue in the ruins outside!" said Djambo. "Except it wasn't a statue."

The beast bowed and growled. "My Emperor Ko!"

Next came a mass of woolly fur. In the

middle was a face with glistening eyes. It hopped to Ko, leaving slimy spots along the floor behind it.

Max winced. "I remember him, too."

Next came a twin-beaked bird. Trailing it was a beast with five tusks, two up, three down.

Ko's three large eyes blazed like fire.

"More! More!" he bellowed.

"Less . . . less . . ." Neal whispered.

But more came.

Beasts of every size and description stomped and waddled and thudded into the palace, taking their place and bowing before Ko.

The Viper had woken them all from sleep.

"My beasts!" shouted the bull-headed ruler, gazing from one creature to another. "This Viper shall wake more of you, all over Droon. We shall cover this world! A new horned tower shall rise from Jaffa City! I shall rule!"

Eric felt trembling next to him. He turned to see Keeah shuddering. "We have to do something," he said. "Stop this."

"Stop it how?" whispered Julie. "Your sparks blast your own toes!"

"Our sparks *do* blast themselves," said Keeah. "But if we know that, and aim carefully . . ."

Eric watched Ko move between a set of giant pillars.

He began to smile. "Let's try it. . . ."

Djambo crawled over and grabbed Sparr's gloves. "If you are going for the Viper, take these. They will protect you."

Eric grinned. "Thanks. Everybody ready?"

Neal's eyes were wide. "Not exactly —"

"Now!"

Blam! BLAM! Eric and Keeah blasted bright silver and violet sparks together.

Even as Ko bellowed, the blasts shot to the ceiling, then curved back at the two running wizards.

"Keeah — jump!" yelled Eric.

Zzzzeeeooooorr — booom! The columns on both sides of Ko exploded before he could move, showering him with large stones. He swatted them away, but his golden crown tumbled from his head. It clattered to the floor.

Eric slid across the stones and grabbed it. The moment he did, the Viper's eyes began to glow.

Ko roared. "Clinkface, Nobclaws, get them!"

"Get yourself!" boomed a loud voice. "You should be in a cage, you four-fisted, three-eyed horntop!"

The giant doorway was suddenly filled

with the large shape of the bearded king of Droon.

Zello and Relna burst into the room with an army of royal guards, all sparking with a protective spell.

"Mother, Father!" called Keeah.

"No little storm or wingy wasp will stop us!" said Relna. "Now get that Viper out of here!"

"We'll take care of these big boys!" said Zello. "This is a two-club job. Hey, you, Stinkface —"

Ko was enraged. "Ninns! Finish the small-fry!"

"Ha!" shouted Neal. "Nobody finishes the fries while I'm around. Come on, people!"

The Ninns broke from the orange veil, waved their swords at the kids, and charged.

Keeah swung around. "To the tower!"

As Zello, Relna, and the guards took on Ko and his beasts, the Ninns charged up the stairs after the children.

When Keeah reached the top step of the tower, she dashed into the uppermost room. Everyone piled in. Max shut the door and barred it.

It was a small room, perfectly round and pointed at the top.

There were no windows, only a thin stream of light shining from the tip of the ceiling to the floor below.

"Dead end," said Julie. "No exit. Now what? Destroy the Viper?"

"I don't know," said Keeah. "What if we need it to send Ko back?"

"Make a fort!" said Djambo. "We love forts!"

"That we can do!" Keeah sent out a quick blast of sparks. It veered around at two large pillars, tumbling them to the floor. Everyone leaped behind them and faced the door.

"Okay. *Now* what?" asked Neal.

Eric's heart pounded like a drum. He heard the stomping feet of the charging Ninns. Hiding there reminded him of the closet that morning.

Only now, all of his friends were jammed in there with him.

Neal, Julie, and Keeah were on one side. Max and Nelag crouched just behind him. Djambo was right next to him.

"My second game of hide-and-seek today," the Orkin whispered. "Except we're hiding and my own brothers are seeking —"

Eric blinked.

My own brothers.

The red warriors stomped more loudly up the stairs.

That's when Eric knew what to do.

He laughed. "Everything Salamandra

did today helped us. We went to the Orkin village because she knew we needed you, Djambo. For right now. When the Ninns chase us!"

"But Orkins play!" said Djambo. "I can't fight Ninns. I can't fight anyone!"

"Not fight." Eric pulled Sparr's gloves tight. Tattered by the explosion, burned, full of holes as they were, he still had to take the chance. "Nelag, read the protection spell," he said.

"Eric?" said Keeah. "What are you doing?"

"We need to go back. . . ." he whispered.

"Go back where?" said Max. "Downstairs?"

Eric held up the Viper. "No. In time —"

Thump! Thump! The Ninns were almost there.

"This is crazy!" said Julie.

Even as Nelag read the backward spell

from the scroll, twin streaks of thick blue fog flowed from the Viper's eyes.

The crown quivered. It burned in Eric's hands.

He almost smiled. "Oven mitts," he said. "Salamandra told us that things would heat up in Droon. I guess that's sure true!"

Neal gulped loudly. "Eric, do you know what you're doing?"

The sound of stomping feet grew louder. The blue fog whirled faster. Eric felt electricity passing through his hands, up his arms, filling his whole self.

"Not really," he said.

He didn't know what he was doing.

But it was as if he knew everything else. Or *saw* everything else. Everything he had ever done and everywhere he had ever been seemed to be spinning inside his head.

Spinning, like the blue storm in the room.

He felt himself falling back into his own past.

He saw his house, his yard, a school bus. Sounds drifted in and out, sing-along songs, his mother's words. There was his father flying him around the room. His first haircut —

Suddenly — *BOOOOM-M-M-M!*

Light exploded in the room, the fog vanished, and Eric fell to the floor, dropping the Viper. An instant later, the door flew open and dozens of warriors in black armor piled into the room. The light from a hundred torches shone off a hundred jagged blades.

And a hundred iron helmets.

And a hundred blue faces.

"Orkins!" shouted Djambo, bursting up and hugging them. "Brothers! Friends!"

"Eric, you did it!" cried Max, helping him up. "You returned the Ninns to the time before they were Ninns. To the time when they were Orkins —"

Blam! Ko burst to the top of the stairs and into the room. He growled at the top of his lungs.

"You children will pay for this! All of Droon will pay —"

Ko reached out an arm and grabbed the Viper from the floor. When he turned back, the whole room of Orkins was standing between him and the friends.

Growling again, his three black eyes burning, his horns flaring and flaming, Ko punched a massive hole through the tower wall and hurled himself to the ground.

Ten

A Misty Moisty Morning

The friends and the Orkins charged down the tower stairs. By the time they raced from the palace, Ko had leaped on the back of the gruffle and was calling his army.

"Kinjah-preth-no-tah!"

One after another his winged and hoofed beasts abandoned the battle with the king and queen and tramped to their leader. Turning, the emperor led his terrible army away into the darkening mist.

Relna and Zello rushed to the friends.

"Ko and his beasts are back in our world now," said Relna. "Thanks to Sparr —"

Fwooosh! There came a sudden streak of green from the jungle shadows, and Salamandra limped out, breathing hard.

"Do not try to stop me!" she hissed.

Eric lowered his hands. "You knew all this would happen," he said.

"Tell us," said Keeah, "will we defeat Ko? And Sparr, too?"

Salamandra stared at the children. She grinned suddenly. "I haven't been that far into the future . . . not yet!"

Then, scattering thorns behind her, she ran after the beasts. Within a few moments, she had vanished into the island mists.

"We're just letting her follow Ko?" asked Neal.

Eric watched the thorn princess vanish. "Salamandra made sure we came to Droon today. She made sure we saw what we did and did what we did. She doesn't like Ko. But maybe she's not an enemy of ours, either."

"That makes sense!" said Nelag. "And so does this!" He ran off and returned a few minutes later, waving the flagpole of Droon over his shoulder. "Come, now. The island will soon leave us!"

King Zello laughed. "Are you saying we need to leave the island now?"

Nelag nodded. "Exactly wrong!"

With a sharp rumble, the ground beneath them shuddered. Then a large, spiky head burst out of the sea offshore. It wrinkled its scaly neck and turned away. The Isle of Mists turned with it.

"Ko wasn't the only thing to wake up!" yelped Djambo. "This whole island is on the back of a serpent!"

Zello boomed. "Come, everyone, to the *Jaffa Wind*. And hurry!"

"Before the island swims away!" chirped Max.

With a great rush, everyone raced down the misty hill to the shore. Once they charged on board the *Jaffa Wind*, the ship rose on a giant wave. No sooner did it crash straight through the storm and into daylight, than the Isle of Mists itself slithered away, taking its fierce twisting winds with it.

"Buh-bye, hurricane!" said Neal. "See you never. I hope!"

As the ship drove north over the waves, they left the Serpent Sea for the great ocean of Droon, sailing past a world of glistening valleys, ice-topped mountains, and silvery rivers.

Eric sighed. "Ko wants to turn all this into his rotten Empire of Shadows? To make this beautiful world as stinky as the Isle of Mists?"

Neal shrugged. "Makes you wish for the good old days of Sparr, doesn't it?"

"Maybe that's the thing about shadows," said Keeah. "You can't have them without the sun!"

As if on cue, the bright pink and blue domes of Jaffa City peeped over the distant horizon, gleaming in the sun of the new day.

Max chuckled. "We turned Ninns into Orkins today. Wouldn't it be great if for every bad thing that Ko does, a good thing might happen, too?"

"Many good things!" said Djambo. "Just look at those climbing ropes. Up, my brothers! Up!"

The new Orkins whooped as they climbed the rigging and hoisted the Droon flag high.

"We must keep Droon safe," said Relna.

"Happily, we have more friends in Droon right now than ever before —"

A sudden whimper sounded behind them.

Everyone turned to see a small dog pop its head out of the shadows at the back of the ship.

A second head lifted up and joined it.

"Oh, my gosh, it's Kem," gasped Keeah. "And he's a puppy! The Viper must have zapped him!"

Neal crouched to the deck. "Here, boy, here —"

But Kem turned back to the shadows and sniffed at a heap of twisted cloth lying there. Pulling hard, he tugged the covering away.

Eric felt his blood go cold.

Underneath the cloth was a small boy. His eyes blinked in the sunshine. His face was as pale as snow, his features wrinkled in fear. He huddled inside a long black tunic that was smeared and torn.

And he wiggled the two small fins behind his ears.

"I can't believe it!" said Keeah. "Sparr? Is that . . . *you?*"

"This can't be true," said Julie. "It's not possible —"

For what seemed like forever, the boy said nothing. Finally, he whispered. "Take me with you . . . please . . . help me. . . ."

Eric's heart thundered in his chest. "It *is* possible. Nelag's old firework exploded at the very moment the Viper was waking up Ko —"

"Quite right!" said the pretend wizard. "Fizzling Fizzlers are the best!"

"The explosion must have turned Sparr back to the age he was when Ko put himself to sleep . . ." said Eric.

The boy shivered. "Take me away from

Ko. . . . I know what he will do. . . . I know his plans. . . . I can help you. . . . please!"

His fins were as small as if they had just started to grow.

Sparr! As a child! thought Eric.

All of a sudden — *whoosh!* — the air lit up.

The rainbow-colored steps of the magic staircase appeared near the ship, floating over the waves.

"Children, you'd better go now," said Queen Relna solemnly, still staring at the boy. "We must get Sparr to Jaffa City at once."

"Home!" boomed the king. "The sail, there! Ho! Quickly! Quickly!"

Eric turned to Keeah. "This changes everything," he whispered.

"We'll be back soon," said Julie.

"Sooner than soon!" added Neal.

"I'll need you," said Keeah.

Even as the three friends jumped to the stairs, and the ship raced away over the waves, they couldn't take their eyes off Sparr, looking up at Keeah in fear.

Or off Keeah, staring back in stunned surprise.

Eric remembered then what Sparr had told them.

"A great new adventure begins."

It sure does, he thought. *But where it will end, no one knows.*

As his friends ran up the stairs ahead of him, Eric remembered something else, too. Shoving his hand in his pocket, he pulled out what he had put there when no one was looking.

The little wooden bird he found in Ko's palace.

Eric stared at the bird.

It stared right back at him.

Errrriccccc!

THE SECRETS OF DROON

by by Tony Abbott

Under the stairs, a magical world awaits yo

$3.99 each!

Available Wherever You Buy Books or Use This Order Form

www.scholastic.com   **SCHOLASTIC**